Billie B. Brown

Billie B. Brown Books

The Bad Butterfly
The Soccer Star
The Midnight Feast
The Second-best Friend
The Extra-special Helper
The Beautiful Haircut
The Big Sister
The Spotty Vacation
The Birthday Mix-up
The Secret Message
The Little Lie
The Best Project
The Deep End
The Copycat Kid
The Night Fright
The Bully Buster
The Missing Tooth
The Book Buddies
The Grumpy Neighbor
The Honey Bees
The Hat Parade

First American Edition 2021
Kane Miller, A Division of EDC Publishing
Original Title: Billie B Brown: *The Grumpy Neighbour*
Text copyright © 2020 Sally Rippin
Illustration copyright © 2020 Aki Fukuoka
Series design copyright 2020 Hardie Grant Egmont
First published in Australia by Hardie Grant Egmont

For information contact:
Kane Miller, A Division of EDC Publishing
P.O. Box 470663
Tulsa, OK 74147-0663
www.kanemiller.com
www.usbornebooksandmore.com

Library of Congress Control Number: 2020937655

Printed and bound in the United States of America
1 2 3 4 5 6 7 8 9 10

ISBN: 978-1-68464-218-2

Billie B. Brown

The Grumpy Neighbor

By Sally Rippin

Illustrated by Aki Fukuoka

Kane Miller

A DIVISION OF EDC PUBLISHING

Chapter One

Billie B. Brown has two shin guards, one stripy soccer top and three new friends to play with. Do you know what the "B" in Billie B. Brown stands for?

Ball!

Billie and Jack are playing soccer. Jack is Billie's best friend. He lives next door. Today Billie and Jack are visiting Jack's cousins. His cousins have a park right next to their house.

Billie brought her brand-new soccer ball. She can't wait to try it out!

One soccer ball

One stripy soccer top

Two shin guards

Jack is on Billie's team.
David and Stella are
on the other team.
Ivy is the goalkeeper.
They kick Billie's new
ball around the park.
It is super bouncy.

"Over here!" yells Jack.
The ball bounces right
off his head. It goes **up**,
up, **up** into the sky.

The ball lands on the
other side of a fence.
Uh-oh!

"I'll get it!" Billie yells.

"No! Stop!" David and Stella shout together.

"Don't climb that fence!"

"Why not?" Billie asks.

Stella looks at David. David looks at Stella. They both look worried.

"That's Grumpy Gertie's house," Stella whispers.

David nods. "No one ever gets their ball back if it goes over her fence," he says.

"Grumpy Gertie is
the meanest person
on our street," says Stella.

Billie laughs.
"Don't be silly," she says.
"I will just knock
on her door and ask
for my ball back.
Are you going to
come with me, Jack?"

Jack shrugs. He looks **scared**. But he follows Billie as far as the front gate.

"We warned you!" David yells.

Billie rolls her eyes at Jack. "They are being very silly!" she snorts. "How mean can she be?"

She walks up to the front door and knocks loudly. She is very brave, isn't she?

Chapter Two

Billie waits on the
front step. She can
hear someone inside.
"She's probably just old,"
Billie says to Jack.
"Some kids find old
people scary. But I don't."

Billie hears the sound of footsteps. She starts to get a teensy bit **nervous**.

Suddenly the door swings open. A short lady with frizzy hair stands on the doorstep. She has a very frowny face. When she sees Billie, she frowns even more. "What do you want?" she says.

"Hello," Billie says in her most polite voice. "My ball went over your fence. Would you mind if I fetch it?"

The lady takes a deep breath. She puffs out her chest. Her face turns very red. She is not very big, but she looks very scary.

"No!" she shouts.
"Every day you kids
kick balls over my fence.
Every day they land in
my garden. Take your
games to another park!"

Billie gasps. "But … but
… it was an accident!" she
says. "That's my new ball!"

"I don't care!" the
lady shouts. "Go away."

She slams the door shut.

Billie runs to meet

Jack at the gate.
She feels **shaky**.

No one has ever shouted at her like that before! "Wow," she says quietly. "She really is mean!"

Billie follows Jack back to the park.

"Sorry about your ball," David says. "We already lost three balls over Grumpy Gertie's fence."

"You will never get it back now," Stella says.

"She's the meanest neighbor ever!" says Ivy.

Billie frowns. Now her
shaky feelings are
turning into **mad**
feelings. She feels
her cheeks get hot.
"That's not fair," she says.
"That's my new ball!"

Oh dear! Poor Billie.
What can she do?

Chapter Three

Billie's dad picks up Jack
and Billie to take them
home. Her baby brother is
asleep in the car. Jack and
Billie slide into the back
seat beside Noah.

"Hey, Nozy!" Billie says quietly. She kisses him on his soft, round nose. Billie **loves** her baby brother. Especially when he's sleeping.

"How was your day?"
Billie's dad asks.

"**Terrible!**" says Billie.
She crosses her arms
against her chest
and frowns.

"Oh, what happened?"
her dad asks.

"She lost her new ball,"
Jack says.

"I didn't lose it," Billie grumbles. "Grumpy Gertie took it!" She tells her dad the whole story. "She's the meanest neighbor ever."

"Oh dear!" Billie's dad says. "Don't worry. Guess what I have for you in the trunk? A box of seedlings to plant!"

"Yay!" Billie says, feeling happy again. She has been wanting to have her own vegetable patch **FOREVER.**

Jack goes next door. Billie follows her dad out into the backyard. He has already dug up the dirt, ready for their new vegetables.

"You can start planting them," says Billie's dad. "I will go and get the compost."

Her dad puts the
seedlings on the ground.

Billie pulls the little
plants out of the box
one by one. Baby plants
are very fragile. Billie is
gentle with them. She
digs little holes in the
dirt and puts them in.

Then she carefully pats
the earth around them.

Noah has woken from
his nap. He crawls across
the grass towards Billie.

"**Mom!**" Billie yells. "Can you get Noah? He's going to wreck my garden."

Billie's dad comes over with the wheelbarrow. "Watch out, Billie!" he calls. "Behind you."

Uh-oh!

Billie spins around. "Noah!" she yells. But she is too late.

Noah has pulled out all of Billie's little plants.

Oh dear! What a mess. Pumpkin, pea, and parsnip plants everywhere!

All Billie's hard work is destroyed. "Noah!" she yells again.

Billie's mom rushes over. "I'm sorry! He was only trying to help," she says. Noah holds out his fists full of dirt towards Billie.

"Look what he's done!" Billie yells.

Noah begins to cry.

"This is the worst day
ever!" Billie shouts.
Then she bursts into tears.

Billie runs into the house.
She rushes upstairs and
flops onto her bed.

Chapter Four

Soon Billie hears a knock
on her bedroom door.
"Billie?" her mom calls.
"Can we come in?"

Billie sits up and wipes
her tears away.

Her mom comes in with Noah. His hands and face have been washed.

"Noah wants to give you something," she says. Noah looks up at Billie with his big round eyes. Then he holds out his hand. In his hand is his favorite teddy. Billie knows this is his way of saying **sorry**.

"Thank you, Noah,"
Billie says. She feels bad
for making her little
brother cry. She opens
up her arms. Noah jumps
onto the bed and gives
Billie the biggest hug ever.

Billie's mom sits next to her. "Dad has planted your seedlings again," she says. "Only a few were broken. The rest will be fine. And now he is building a greenhouse to protect them from Noah."

"Oh, that's a great idea!" says Billie.

"Naughty Noah," she says. But she is smiling. She feels **much better** now that everything is fixed. And she knows Noah didn't mean to wreck her garden.

"Dad told me about your soccer ball, too," her mom says.

"That lady wouldn't give it back to me," Billie frowns. She feels **cross** again. "She is so mean. That was my new ball!"

"I understand," Billie's mom says. "But maybe she really loves her garden, too? Imagine what happens when a ball goes over her fence. It probably bounces all over her plants and crushes them."

"Oh!" says Billie. "I didn't think of that." She knows exactly how that must feel.

Billie looks at Noah's teddy in her lap. And suddenly she has an idea. A **super-duper** idea.

"Mom! I think I know how to get my ball back," she says, grinning.

"But I'll need Dad's help. Do you think he can drive me back to that house?"

"I'm sure he can," says her mom. "But what's your plan?"

Billie smiles. "I'll tell you later," she says. She runs out of the room.

Can you guess what she is up to?

Before long, Billie and her dad arrive at the house. Billie stands on the doorstep with her dad. He is carrying some bits and pieces to build a greenhouse.

Billie carries a box of seedlings. She has picked out all her favorite vegetables.

She hopes Gertie
likes pumpkin, peas,
and parsnip!

This time when she
knocks, Billie is not
nervous at all.

Billie B. Brown — The Bad Butterfly
By Sally Rippin

Billie B. Brown — The Soccer Star
By Sally Rippin

Billie B. Brown — The Midnight Feast
By Sally Rippin

Billie B. Brown — The Second-best Friend
By Sally Rippin

Billie B. Brown — The Extra-special Helper
By Sally Rippin

Billie B. Brown — The Beautiful Haircut
By Sally Rippin

Billie B. Brown — The Big Sister
By Sally Rippin

Billie B. Brown — The Spotty Vacation
By Sally Rippin

Billie B. Brown — The Birthday Mix-up
By Sally Rippin

Billie B. Brown — The Secret Message
By Sally Rippin

Billie B. Brown — The Little Lie
By Sally Rippin

Billie B. Brown — The Best Project
By Sally Rippin

Billie B. Brown — The Deep End
By Sally Rippin

Billie B. Brown — The Copycat Kid
By Sally Rippin

Billie B. Brown — The Night Fright
By Sally Rippin

Billie B. Brown — The Missing Tooth
By Sally Rippin

Billie B. Brown — The Bully Buster
By Sally Rippin

Billie B. Brown — The Grumpy Neighbor
By Sally Rippin

Billie B. Brown — The Hat Parade
By Sally Rippin

Billie B. Brown — The Honey Bees
By Sally Rippin

Collect them all!

Don't forget the book starring both Jack AND Billie!

Billie B. Brown & Hey Jack!
The Book Buddies
By Sally Rippin